A Lucky Charm Book

SO-CMP-662

The Shining Star

by Jane P. Resnick
Illustrated by Jael

kidsbooks®
Incorporated

On the night of her birthday, Emily climbed into bed with a happy feeling, laughing about the cake her mother had baked. It was in the shape of a swimming pool, with blue icing for water and licorice strings to mark racing lanes. Emily was on the town swim team and loved the water.

"Boy, everyone dove into that cake," her father said afterwards, making another one of his corny jokes. Emily had to admit that her friends did gobble it up.

Her mother knocked softly on the door and came in. "Hi, birthday girl," she said. "I have one last present for you. I saved the best for last."

She sat down on the bed and handed Emily a blue velvet box, the kind jewelers use. It looked old and worn around the corners, as if it had been opened many times.

"Oh!" Emily gasped when she looked inside. There was a charm bracelet made of a small silver chain and one perfect, shining star. Emily hugged her mother. "How beautiful!"

"And it's very special, too," her mother said. "My grandmother gave this star to my mother, your grandmother, Nana. Nana gave it to me, and now it's yours. It's a wishing star."

"Really?" Emily said, taking it out of the box.

"Yes," her mother said softly. "But only for wishes that are really important. It's not meant for silly, selfish wishes, so you must choose your wishes carefully."

"What do you mean?" Emily asked. "If I wish for something, I want it. Isn't that selfish?"

"No," her mother said, "not if it's a generous wish from the heart."

"How will I know?" Emily asked.

Her mother thought a moment. Then she said quietly, "Nana always said you were special. She said you would know. And I agree with her."

Emily thought of her grandmother. She wore her black-and-white hair in old-fashioned braids across the top of her head. Once Emily saw her at night in her purple robe with her long braids undone. Her hair was amazing, glowing around her face and falling down her back. She looked like a queen in stories of ancient times. She was like the wise old woman you could never fool.

"If Nana said I'd know, I guess I'll figure it out," Emily said. "Thank you." And she hugged her mother goodnight.

The first thing Emily did in the morning was put on her bracelet. The star glittered on her wrist. She watched it twinkle in the mirror when she brushed her teeth, and it made her smile.

Emily combed her straight hair and took a good look at herself in the mirror. "OK," she thought, "except for this old nose." She had a pleasant oval face and round cheeks, but her nose was a little long and thin. Needlenose, her Dad called her when he teased her. He had a nickname for everybody. Emily knew he meant it with affection, but sometimes it bothered her.

"I wish my nose was nicer," she murmured. The little star clinked against the bathroom tile. "Uh oh," Emily thought. "Nana would think that was a silly wish for sure. Forget it. This nose will do."

Emily wore her bracelet to school and showed it to her teacher, Miss Norris. The kids called her Nurse Norris behind her back. It was her voice. Emily's friend Billy could imitate her perfectly. He'd take a deep breath and make his voice really high. "Yes, dear," he'd say in a sing-song, cheery lilt just like a nurse talking to a patient. Just like Miss Norris.

"How lovely, dear!" Miss Norris chirped, admiringly. "It reminds me of the poem, 'Star bright, star light, first star I see tonight. I wish I may, I wish I might, have the wish I wish tonight.'"

"That's true," Emily answered. But she didn't tell Miss Norris about real wishing. That seemed like a family secret.

At that very moment, important wishes were being made by another member of Emily's family, someone that she didn't know anything about. Her cousin, Isabelle, who lived in Paris, was looking up at the night sky and wishing—very hard.

"Star bright, star light," she said, "first star I see tonight . . . I wish I had a real home and friends of my own." She closed her eyes and took a deep breath. It was the same wish she made every night.

Isabelle was an American girl who lived with her father. Because she had come to Paris as a small child, she spoke English and French. Her father traveled a lot because of his job, and Isabelle often went with him. Instead of going to a regular school, she had an "au pair," a young woman who took care of her and acted as her tutor.

Hotels were where Isabelle spent most of her time, and she could get along in them just like they were her own backyard. She knew how to call room service and order her favorite French dessert, crepe suzette. She knew how to call housekeeping if there were no towels and the bell captain if her suitcase got left in the lobby. But Isabelle had no one her own age to be with, and she was very

12

lonely. Isabelle's wish was a real wish from the heart.

Isabelle heard the door of the hotel suite close. It was her father coming in. She turned on her light.

"Hello, sweetheart. Not sleeping?" he asked, walking to the bed.

"No," she sighed. "I was wishing."

"For what?" he inquired, bending over to give her a hug.

"Just wishing," Isabelle answered.

"Well, I have a surprise," he said. "We're going to America for the summer."

"We are? Why?" Isabelle asked.

"I have business there. I will have to travel a lot, all over the United States," her father replied.

"Oh," Isabelle said. Her face clouded over.

"But, you won't," he said. "You're going to stay with Aunt Louise and Uncle Jim in Somerset, Massachusetts. Your cousin Emily is just your age, so you'll have someone to be with. Summers in America are great," he went on. "There are barbecues and swimming. And, where your uncle and aunt live, there's even an amusement park nearby."

"But I don't know them," Isabelle cried. She slid down and pulled the covers up to her nose.

"Well, when you get to know them, I'm sure you'll like them," her father said kindly. "Now go to sleep. We'll talk about it tomorrow." He kissed Isabelle goodnight and shut off the light.

"Staying with strangers!" Isabelle thought. Hotel rooms didn't seem so bad after all. She wondered what Aunt Louise and Uncle Jim and Emily looked like. She tried to remember family pictures, but all she could think of was her grandmother, Nana, with her black-and-white hair and her braids across the top of her head.

Isabelle's and her father's arrival from Paris was a great reunion for the grown-ups. He and Emily's mother were brother and sister, so they were happy to see one another. But her father only stayed a few days, then left for a long business trip.

Isabelle felt like crying when he said good-bye. She was terrified of being left with strangers. Isabelle wanted to tell her father that she was afraid, but she didn't want to disappoint him.

"Je t'aime," he said. "I love you. I'll call you all the time."

Isabelle felt more alone now than ever.

The first thing everyone noticed about Isabelle was her hair. It was a delightful golden color. And there was lots of it—curls and curls and more curls.

Emily's Dad found a nickname for Isabelle right away. "What gorgeous honey-colored hair you have, Honey Bun," he said. "You'll have to watch out for honey bears. . .and boys."

Isabelle giggled and ducked her head. Her curls bounced and caught all the light around them. She liked Uncle Jim right away. He tried to be funny, and even if he wasn't, she could tell he meant to be kind.

Emily scowled. "Honey Bun," she thought

irritably. "That's a lot better than Needlenose.
I guess Dad didn't notice that Isabelle is kind of
short. *Shrimp* is more like it."

Emily still had four weeks of school
before summer vacation. Since Isabelle's
tutor didn't come to America, she had to go to
Emily's class. On the school bus the first
morning, Emily's best friend, Lydia, got on
and sat behind them.

"How ya' doing?" Lydia asked Emily.
Emily nodded and shrugged. Before Isabelle
had arrived, Lydia had promised Emily she

would help her with her cousin.

"Hi! Isabelle, right?" Lydia said.

"Hi," Isabelle said shyly.

"Wow! Great hair," Lydia said, admiring Isabelle's curls. "Do you curl it?"

"*Mais non,*" Isabelle answered, forgetting to speak English. "Uh. . .no," she said, touching her hair with a delicate pat. "It's natural."

"My father calls it honey-colored," Emily said, in a voice that sounded strange to Lydia. She gave Emily a confused look.

"What kind of sports do you play in France?" Lydia asked.

"I don't play anything," Isabelle answered hesitantly.

"Want me to teach you basketball?" Lydia inquired.

"Sure," Isabelle replied, happy to be included.

"Emily won't play with me," Lydia said. "All she cares about is swimming."

It was true. Emily wasn't good at basket-ball and didn't like it. But she didn't want Lydia to spend that much time with Isabelle. Lydia was *her* best friend.

"So," she heard Lydia say to Isabelle, "how about after school?"

What happened when Emily walked into her classroom with Isabelle was just what she had expected. Everyone was watching them.

"This is my cousin Isabelle," she said to Miss Norris at the teacher's desk. Emily could feel eyes staring at her from all around the room. "She's staying with me."

"Of course," Miss Norris said. "I've spoken with your father about her visit. How long will you be staying?" she asked Isabelle with a friendly smile.

"For the summer," Isabelle answered quietly. "I live in Paris."

"Oh? Do you speak French?" Miss Norris asked in her perkiest nurse's voice. The teacher looked at Isabelle as if she were a prize she had won at a carnival.

"*Oui,*" Isabelle nodded, her curls bobbing.

"Speak English," Emily hissed. More kids were coming into the room and they were all staring.

"Oh, no, Emily," Miss Norris said. "It's

wonderful to speak a second language at a young age. I adore French. *Je parle francais un peu,* I speak a little French myself," she said, beaming at Isabelle.

"*Tres bien,*" Isabelle replied smiling. "Your accent is very good."

"We'd better sit down," Emily said. Her cheeks were starting to feel hot. She nudged Isabelle toward a seat near hers.

She could hear Billy laughing at the back of the room. "Ooh, la, la," he snickered. "Hey, Emily, I've got an empty seat for your cousin next to me."

"Four weeks of this!" Emily thought. "Why couldn't school be over sooner?"

At lunch, Billy tried to sit next to Isabelle, but Emily quickly sat down on one side of Isabelle and Lydia on the other. Isabelle looked at her plate. The spaghetti and meatballs lay next to a big square of green jello. She scrunched up her face.

"Ugly stuff, huh," Lydia said to Isabelle.

"What's your favorite food?"

"Crepe suzette," she answered right away. "I always order them from room service."

"Brownies are my favorite," Emily interrupted too loudly.

"They're everybody's," Lydia snapped, barely turning her head. "What's a suzette, Isabelle? Who serves you in your room?"

The whole table was waiting for her answer.

"It's like a pancake with delicious orange syrup," Isabelle explained.

"Wow!" Lydia said. "They sound terrific."

Lydia was paying so much attention to Isabelle that she didn't even notice she was dripping red tomato sauce all over her shirt.

Emily stopped listening. She stabbed her jello and thought of how great it would be if Isabelle's favorite food was white bread without crust.

After school the next day, Emily and Isabelle walked over to the town pool for swim practice. Emily liked being on the swim team, but mostly she loved being in the water, where she felt strong and graceful. Isabelle wasn't so sure about swimming. She could swim. But race? She felt that getting along here meant facing a new test every day.

Emily was glad to introduce Isabelle to Coach Peters. Honey-colored curls and French words wouldn't mean a thing to him. All he cared about was swimming.

"Can you do freestyle?" Coach asked Isabelle. "We could sure use a freestyler in your age-group."

"Is that the crawl?" Isabelle asked.

"Yup, your basic stroke," he answered.

"That's all I can do," Isabelle said.

"Good enough," Coach said. "In the water. Let's go."

Emily went off to practice her stroke, the butterfly. She pretended she was a dolphin curving and dipping into the ocean. She wished she could swim faster, but hard as she tried, she always slowed down at the end of a race. When Emily came out of the water, Isabelle was walking toward her with Coach Peters, who was patting her on the shoulder.

"Your cousin is a natural, Emily," he said. "She's not fast yet, but she will be. Just what the team needs. Sent from heaven."

Isabelle smiled. Emily dove back into the water and stayed under for a long time.

That night Emily made up her mind to be nice to Isabelle. She realized it wasn't Isabelle's fault that everyone found her so fascinating. The girls were sharing Emily's room. When they got ready for bed, Emily showed her bracelet with the star to Isabelle.

"*Tres jolie.* Oops. Sorry. It's beautiful," Isabelle said.

"It's for wishing," Emily explained. "But only from the heart, not selfish wishes. I'm not sure what that means, though. I wish that

people weren't hungry or homeless. I know *that* isn't a selfish wish." She paused and thought for a minute "But I think the star is for personal wishes."

"Star light, star bright," Isabelle said looking at the sparkling silver star. "I have a personal wish."

"You do?" Emily asked. "What is it?"

"Well. . ." Isabelle said. It was hard to admit what she really wanted. The words stuck in her throat and made her feel like crying. "I guess. . .it's . . .uh. . .a secret."

"Oh," Emily snapped. She snatched back her bracelet. "How," she thought, "could she be friends with someone who kept secrets?"

Emily was beginning to wish that Isabelle had never come to America, but she knew that wasn't very nice. Actually, she felt like wishing that Isabelle was stuck on top of the Eiffel Tower with no way down. But then the image of her grandmother popped into her mind.

"I'm sorry, Nana," she thought. "It's hard not to have selfish wishes with Isabelle around. I'd like to have honey-colored curls and speak French and have everybody go googly-eyed over me, too. But the way it is, all I have is straight hair, a needlenose, and boring old English."

Once school was out for the summer, the girls fell into a routine. Emily went to a special art class in the mornings, and Lydia often invited Isabelle over to play basketball. She had a hoop on her garage. When Isabelle made her first basket, she was so excited that she jumped into the air and shouted *"Voila!"* (VWAH-LA) which means, "Look at this!" or "Here it is!"

The word amused Lydia, and she and Isabelle said it all the time, like an inside joke. It made Emily feel left out and she fumed. Lydia was spending more time with Isabelle than she was with her.

In the afternoons, the girls went to swim practice. There were several swim meets and, as Coach had predicted, Isabelle's times improved greatly. Coach made a big fuss over her. He had his eye on the league championship, and Isabelle became his secret weapon, the new kid no one knew about. But the better Isabelle did, the worse Emily seemed to swim. She kept watching Isabelle out of the corner of her eye. By the middle of August, Isabelle was winning races and Emily was slipping from her usual second place to an occasional third.

The team did make it to the championships—Somerset against Westfield. Isabelle and Emily were to swim their usual individual events, as well as the medley relay. In the relay, a race that requires team effort, four girls would each swim two laps. Susan would swim the backstroke, Emily the butterfly, Molly the breaststroke, and Isabelle the freestyle.

The relay became the crucial race. Winning it would bring in the points Somerset needed to clinch the trophy.

Standing behind the starting block, the girls tingled with nervousness. They shook their arms and legs, dancing up and down. Bam! The gun went off, and the backstrokers arched away from the side, arms windmilling.

Emily stepped onto the block. The butter-

fly was next. The moment that Susan returned she had to dive in. Hesitating would cost the team valuable seconds. Emily looked back at Isabelle. "She's going to do better than me," she thought, and for that minute she forgot to watch Susan.

"EMILY!" she heard Coach shouting her name. She turned around and there was Susan panting at the edge of the pool. She had finished her laps and was staring at Emily.

"Oh, no!" Emily thought and dove into the water. She was so upset she couldn't get her stroke right. The harder she tried, the slower she seemed to go. When she finished she knew she had ruined the team's chance. She went right to the bench and sat down without looking at anyone.

Somerset was behind, but Molly swam a good breaststroke and made up some time. Isabelle stood shaking on the block waiting to start, watching the other team's freestyler get a big head start. She dove in and began swimming faster than anyone had ever seen her go. She was like a shark knifing through the water with hardly a splash. At the turn she was gaining on the other swimmer.

Everyone was standing up and screaming. No one could believe that she was catching up. By the middle of the second lap, the two swimmers were even. They were head-to-head until the last second when Isabelle's arm stretched forward and touched the finish!

The whole team mobbed Isabelle, jumping and cheering. Everybody was hugging

one another. Except Emily. She got up from the bench and walked unnoticed into the locker room.

"We won! *C'est fantastique!* How wonderful!" Isabelle cried, rushing into the locker room.

"You won," Emily blurted.

"The team won," Isabelle said, confused. "Isn't it great?"

"Yeah, well, you're Queen of the Day," Emily yelled, slamming her locker. "You think you're so great. You took my friends! You even have to swim better than me."

"What do you mean?" Isabelle said, shocked. She stood very still. With her hair wet and matted to her head she looked small and afraid. Tears began to form in her eyes.

"Everybody thinks you're so hot," Emily said in a low voice. "But I wish you'd go back to where you came from. To France, where everybody speaks French." Emily's voice began to crack. "To your hotels and your

room service and your crepe suzette. That's what I wish." She grabbed her gym bag and stomped out of the locker room.

Emily's mother and father were waiting for them in the car. The girls climbed in with stony faces.

"Congratulations!" Emily's mother said, smiling.

"Champions! All right!" her father chimed in. "Let's celebrate."

The silence in the back seat was noticeable. Emily's Mom and Dad glanced at each other but kept talking.

"We've got a surprise for you," Emily's father said. "We know a nice French restaurant in Westfield. Would you like to go there?" Emily didn't say a thing.

"Oh, yes," Isabelle replied. She didn't want to be rude. "Thank you."

When they got to the restaurant, Emily's father took the waiter aside and spoke to him. The man winked and nodded.

"*Bonsoir.* Good evening, *mademoiselles,*" he smiled at the girls. "What can I get for you?"

"Get me out of here," Emily thought.

"You're going to love this food, Honey Bun," Emily's father said to Isabelle. "And you, too, Needle. . ." Something in Emily's expression made him stop short.

There was a big fuss about ordering. Emily said "fine" in a toneless voice to everything that her father suggested. Isabelle

answered questions about French food as if she were taking a test.

"Exactly what is *foie gras?*" Emily's mother asked.

"Goose liver," Isabelle answered.

"Gross!" Emily barked.

When the main course arrived, everyone concentrated on eating, as if conversation wasn't permitted at meals. Her father didn't even tell Emily to take her elbows off the table. When the dishes were cleared, Emily's mother broke the silence.

"Girls," she began, "I have something to say." Then she hesitated. "I'm really proud of you both. Isabelle, you did a hard thing coming here to stay with us all by yourself. I know it was lonely at first, but you were very brave. I've always wanted Emily to have a sister," she went on, "and I wish it could be you. We'll hate to see you go."

"Emily," she continued, looking lovingly at her daughter. "You're the one who made Isabelle feel like part of the family, taking her to school and sharing all your friends with her. I know it wasn't easy for you either. Dad and I knew you could do it. You're the best."

Emily didn't know what to say. She opened her mouth, but just then the waiter came to the table with a flaming copper pan.

"*Voila!*" he said. "Crepe suzette!"

"Oooh!" Isabelle cried. "*Merci, merci!* Thank you, thank you!"

W hen the girls got back home and went to their room, they both started talking at once.

"I'm sorry," Emily blurted out.

"I'm an idiot," Isabelle said.

Their words crossed and they both started giggling with relief.

"I was being selfish. . .and jealous," Emily admitted.

"I didn't know how to act," Isabelle confessed. "I never had any friends. I've always been alone. I wish I had a family like yours. I wish. . .I wish. . .I could stay here with you."

"Really?" Emily said slowly.

"Yes," Isabelle said. "That was my secret wish. I think of it every night. Star light, star bright. . .that's my wish."

Emily went to her drawer and took out the velvet box with her bracelet and its shining star. She closed her hand around the little star. "That sounds like a real wish to me," she said.

The next day, Emily told her mother about Isabelle's wish. "Do you think we could get her a bracelet like mine with a star for wishing?" she asked.

"What a good idea," her mother said, putting her arm around Emily. "But remember, wishing doesn't always make things come true. Isabelle's father will be back soon. It will be up to him."

Emily's mother got a bracelet for Isabelle that looked exactly like Emily's. On the night before Isabelle's father returned, Emily gave it to her. They were in their room getting ready for bed. Isabelle had been very quiet the last few days. She was upset about leaving, and she looked sad.

"Surprise!" Emily said, as she handed her the box. Isabelle opened it. The little star shone brightly.

"Oh," she breathed. "It's just like yours."

"Yes," Emily said. "It's your *very own* wishing star." And she told Isabelle the story

about her shining star, how it had belonged to Nana and her mother. "You should have one, too," Emily said quietly, "because you're part of our family."

Isabelle smiled gratefully. "I remember a picture of Nana," she said. "It seems funny that she's my grandmother, too. Those braids on top of her head like a crown . . . she looked like a queen."

"She'd think your wish is a good one," Emily told her. "I'll wish on my star that you

43

can stay here and you wish on yours. Maybe it'll come true."

Emily put her arm around Isabelle's shoulders, and they closed their eyes and made their wish. Emily knew that, at last, she had made a generous wish from the heart.

Isabelle's father arrived the next day around dinner time. Isabelle was nervous about telling him her wish. The whole family sat down to a welcome-home dinner, and Isabelle's father described all the places he'd been in the United States.

Finally he said, "Here's the big news. My job is changing. I have a chance to stay in this country. Isabelle and I could live here—right in this neighborhood as a matter of fact. What do you think of that, Sweetheart?"

Isabelle was so excited she could barely speak. "My wish," she gasped. "Daddy, my wish came true!"

"What?" he said.

"Never mind," she answered. "Yes, I

think, yes, *oui*, okay!"

Emily and Isabelle got up from their chairs and danced around in a hug. Isabelle's father looked happily on. Emily's Mom and Dad crept into the kitchen. A few minutes later they came into the room laughing, carrying a flaming pan.

"What's this?" Isabelle's father exclaimed. "Crepe suzette!? No wonder you want to stay here, Isabelle! It's just like home."